THE BOXCAR CHILDREN® MYSTERIES

THE BOXCAR CHILDREN
SURPRISE ISLAND
THE YELLOW HOUSE MYSTERY
MYSTERY RANCH
MIKE'S MYSTERY
BLUE BAY MYSTERY
THE WOODSHED MYSTERY
THE LIGHTHOUSE MYSTERY
MOUNTAIN TOP MYSTERY
SCHOOLHOUSE MYSTERY
CABOOSE MYSTERY
HOUSEBOAT MYSTERY
SNOWBOUND MYSTERY
TREE HOUSE MYSTERY
BICYCLE MYSTERY
MYSTERY IN THE SAND
MYSTERY BEHIND THE WALL
BUS STATION MYSTERY
BENNY UNCOVERS A MYSTERY
THE HAUNTED CABIN MYSTERY
THE DESERTED LIBRARY MYSTERY
THE ANIMAL SHELTER MYSTERY
THE OLD MOTEL MYSTERY
THE MYSTERY OF THE HIDDEN PAINTING
THE AMUSEMENT PARK MYSTERY
THE MYSTERY OF THE MIXED-UP ZOO
THE CAMP-OUT MYSTERY
THE MYSTERY GIRL
THE MYSTERY CRUISE
THE DISAPPEARING FRIEND MYSTERY
THE MYSTERY OF THE SINGING GHOST
THE MYSTERY IN THE SNOW
THE PIZZA MYSTERY
THE MYSTERY HORSE
THE MYSTERY AT THE DOG SHOW
THE CASTLE MYSTERY
THE MYSTERY OF THE LOST VILLAGE
THE MYSTERY ON THE ICE
THE MYSTERY OF THE PURPLE POOL
THE GHOST SHIP MYSTERY
THE MYSTERY IN WASHINGTON, DC
THE CANOE TRIP MYSTERY
THE MYSTERY OF THE HIDDEN BEACH
THE MYSTERY OF THE MISSING CAT
THE MYSTERY AT SNOWFLAKE INN

THE MYSTERY ON STAGE
THE DINOSAUR MYSTERY
THE MYSTERY OF THE STOLEN MUSIC
THE MYSTERY AT THE BALL PARK
THE CHOCOLATE SUNDAE MYSTERY
THE MYSTERY OF THE HOT AIR BALLOON
THE MYSTERY BOOKSTORE
THE PILGRIM VILLAGE MYSTERY
THE MYSTERY OF THE STOLEN BOXCAR
THE MYSTERY IN THE CAVE
THE MYSTERY ON THE TRAIN
THE MYSTERY AT THE FAIR
THE MYSTERY OF THE LOST MINE
THE GUIDE DOG MYSTERY
THE HURRICANE MYSTERY
THE PET SHOP MYSTERY
THE MYSTERY OF THE SECRET MESSAGE
THE FIREHOUSE MYSTERY
THE MYSTERY IN SAN FRANCISCO
THE NIAGARA FALLS MYSTERY
THE MYSTERY AT THE ALAMO
THE OUTER SPACE MYSTERY
THE SOCCER MYSTERY
THE MYSTERY IN THE OLD ATTIC
THE GROWLING BEAR MYSTERY
THE MYSTERY OF THE LAKE MONSTER
THE MYSTERY AT PEACOCK HALL
THE WINDY CITY MYSTERY
THE BLACK PEARL MYSTERY
THE CEREAL BOX MYSTERY
THE PANTHER MYSTERY
THE MYSTERY OF THE QUEEN'S JEWELS
THE STOLEN SWORD MYSTERY
THE BASKETBALL MYSTERY
THE MOVIE STAR MYSTERY
THE MYSTERY OF THE PIRATE'S MAP
THE GHOST TOWN MYSTERY
THE MYSTERY OF THE BLACK RAVEN
THE MYSTERY IN THE MALL
THE MYSTERY IN NEW YORK
THE GYMNASTICS MYSTERY
THE POISON FROG MYSTERY
THE MYSTERY OF THE EMPTY SAFE
THE HOME RUN MYSTERY
THE GREAT BICYCLE RACE MYSTERY

THE MYSTERY OF THE WILD PONIES
THE MYSTERY IN THE COMPUTER GAME
THE HONEYBEE MYSTERY
THE MYSTERY AT THE CROOKED HOUSE
THE HOCKEY MYSTERY
THE MYSTERY OF THE MIDNIGHT DOG
THE MYSTERY OF THE SCREECH OWL
THE SUMMER CAMP MYSTERY
THE COPYCAT MYSTERY
THE HAUNTED CLOCK TOWER MYSTERY
THE MYSTERY OF THE TIGER'S EYE
THE DISAPPEARING STAIRCASE MYSTERY
THE MYSTERY ON BLIZZARD MOUNTAIN
THE MYSTERY OF THE SPIDER'S CLUE
THE CANDY FACTORY MYSTERY
THE MYSTERY OF THE MUMMY'S CURSE
THE MYSTERY OF THE STAR RUBY
THE STUFFED BEAR MYSTERY
THE MYSTERY OF ALLIGATOR SWAMP
THE MYSTERY AT SKELETON POINT
THE TATTLETALE MYSTERY
THE COMIC BOOK MYSTERY
THE GREAT SHARK MYSTERY
THE ICE CREAM MYSTERY
THE MIDNIGHT MYSTERY
THE MYSTERY IN THE FORTUNE COOKIE
THE BLACK WIDOW SPIDER MYSTERY
THE RADIO MYSTERY
THE MYSTERY OF THE RUNAWAY GHOST
THE FINDERS KEEPERS MYSTERY
THE MYSTERY OF THE HAUNTED BOXCAR
THE CLUE IN THE CORN MAZE
THE GHOST OF THE CHATTERING BONES
THE SWORD OF THE SILVER KNIGHT
THE GAME STORE MYSTERY
THE MYSTERY OF THE ORPHAN TRAIN
THE VANISHING PASSENGER
THE GIANT YO-YO MYSTERY
THE CREATURE IN OGOPOGO LAKE
THE ROCK 'N' ROLL MYSTERY
THE SECRET OF THE MASK
THE SEATTLE PUZZLE
THE GHOST IN THE FIRST ROW
THE BOX THAT WATCH FOUND
A HORSE NAMED DRAGON
THE GREAT DETECTIVE RACE
THE GHOST AT THE DRIVE-IN MOVIE

THE MYSTERY OF THE TRAVELING TOMATOES
THE SPY GAME
THE DOG-GONE MYSTERY
THE VAMPIRE MYSTERY
SUPERSTAR WATCH
THE SPY IN THE BLEACHERS
THE AMAZING MYSTERY SHOW
THE PUMPKIN HEAD MYSTERY
THE CUPCAKE CAPER
THE CLUE IN THE RECYCLING BIN
MONKEY TROUBLE
THE ZOMBIE PROJECT
THE GREAT TURKEY HEIST
THE GARDEN THIEF
THE BOARDWALK MYSTERY
THE MYSTERY OF THE FALLEN TREASURE
THE RETURN OF THE GRAVEYARD GHOST
THE MYSTERY OF THE STOLEN SNOWBOARD
THE MYSTERY OF THE WILD WEST BANDIT
THE MYSTERY OF THE SOCCER SNITCH
THE MYSTERY OF THE GRINNING GARGOYLE
THE MYSTERY OF THE MISSING POP IDOL
THE MYSTERY OF THE STOLEN DINOSAUR BONES
THE MYSTERY AT THE CALGARY STAMPEDE
THE SLEEPY HOLLOW MYSTERY
THE LEGEND OF THE IRISH CASTLE
THE CELEBRITY CAT CAPER
HIDDEN IN THE HAUNTED SCHOOL
THE ELECTION DAY DILEMMA
THE DOUGHNUT WHODUNIT
THE ROBOT RANSOM
THE LEGEND OF THE HOWLING WEREWOLF
THE DAY OF THE DEAD MYSTERY
THE HUNDRED-YEAR MYSTERY
THE SEA TURTLE MYSTERY
SECRET ON THE THIRTEENTH FLOOR
THE POWER DOWN MYSTERY
MYSTERY AT CAMP SURVIVAL
THE MYSTERY OF THE FORGOTTEN FAMILY
THE SKELETON KEY MYSTERY
SCIENCE FAIR SABOTAGE
NEW! THE GREAT GREENFIELD BAKE-OFF
NEW! THE BEEKEEPER MYSTERY

THE BOXCAR CHILDREN®

CREATED BY
GERTRUDE CHANDLER WARNER

BOOK

158

THE GREAT GREENFIELD BAKE-OFF

ILLUSTRATED BY
ANTHONY VanARSDALE

ALBERT WHITMAN & COMPANY
CHICAGO, ILLINOIS

ISBN 978-0-8075-0820-6 (hardcover)
ISBN 978-0-8075-0821-3 (paperback)
ISBN 978-0-8075-0822-0 (ebook)

Printed in the United States of America
10 9 8 7 6 5 4 3 2 1 LB 26 25 24 23 22 21

Illustrations by Anthony VanArsdale

Visit The Boxcar Children® online at www.boxcarchildren.com.
For more information about Albert Whitman & Company,
visit our website at www.albertwhitman.com.

Contents

A Contest

"Henry!" Six-year-old Benny came running from the playground, across the green grass. He was shouting his older brother's name. "HENRY! HENRY! HENRY!" In his hand was a yellow piece of paper. He shouted for his sisters too. "JESSIE! VIOLET! JESSIE! VIOLET!"

"What's going on, Benny?" Henry raised his eyes from the book he was reading. The playground was close to where Henry, Violet, and Jessie had laid out their picnic blanket. This spot, under the old oak tree, was perfect for both watching Benny play and resting in the shade.

"The best thing ever is going to happen here in Greenfield!" Benny waved the flyer. He repeated

1

with pure joy, "Best thing ever!"

"Well, are you going to tell us?" Twelve-year-old Jessie was cutting recipes out of a magazine and sorting them into a file box.

"Guess!" Benny challenged. He playfully tucked the flyer behind his back.

"Is it a new mystery?" Violet was ten. She stopped doodling with colored pencils on a drawing pad and studied Benny's face.

The Aldens were known around town for being great detectives.

Henry smiled. "It's been a little while since we solved a mystery."

"Sounds like fun," Jessie agreed.

"That's a good guess," Benny said. He pinched his lips and shook his head. "But it's not a mystery." He laughed. "Want to guess again?"

Henry was fourteen. The others looked to him as if he might know since he was the oldest. "Hmm," Henry rubbed his chin. "Let's see." He rattled off the clues. "Benny is excited. He's holding a yellow flyer. And it's not a mystery." Henry looked at his sisters. "What do those clues mean to you?"

"There's only one thing that Benny likes as much as mysteries," Jessie said with a wink.

The other Alden siblings said in unison, "Food."

Violet laughed so hard her two dark-brown ponytails shook.

"Yes," Henry agreed. "Benny loves eating." He stared at Benny for a long moment then added, "And contests!"

Jessie pushed back a strand of her long brown hair and thought about the possibilities. "It might be an eating contest."

"Remember the hot dog eating competition?" Henry said with a laugh. "Benny ate the most hot dogs and won first place."

"I think," Violet said thoughtfully, "since last year's town competition was a food-eating contest, this year's is probably—"

"A food-making contest?" said Henry.

Jessie turned to Benny and asked, "Is there going to be a baking contest in Greenfield?"

Benny brought the flyer around his back. He handed it to Henry with a smile. "One hundred and ten percent correct," he said. "The Aldens are the best guessers." Then he looked sideways at his family. "But are they the best bakers too?"

"Not me." Henry laughed while running a hand over his thick dark hair. "I burned the toast this morning."

"I'm an artist," Violet said. "I'd rather draw a cake than bake one."

"Jessie can do it!" Benny said. "She made my birthday cake this year." He rubbed his belly. "And it was delicious! My tummy is still saying thank you."

Jessie was up to the challenge. "Tell us what the flyer says," she told Henry. "I could try."

Henry studied the announcement. "It's the Great Greenfield Bake-Off, a baking competition for kids." He checked the rules. "You need two people for a team. Everyone must bake desserts."

"I'll help," Benny said. "I can be the taster!"

"You can't eat everything I make," Jessie told him. "If we're a team, you have to be the sous-chef."

"The soup chef?" Benny licked his lips. "I do love soup."

"Sous," Jessie corrected. "It's a French word. It sounds like *sue*. You don't say the last *s*. The assistant to the main chef is called the sous-chef. For our team, you'd be the second baker in charge."

"I like it!" Benny cheered. "With Benny as sous, Team Alden comes through!" He smiled and said, "It rhymes."

Henry, Jessie, and Violet all chuckled.

"Violet and I will be in the audience," Henry said.

"We can cheer you on," Violet said. "I'll make signs."

Excited about this new adventure, Henry, Jessie, Violet, and Benny went back to their boxcar to get started right away on the perfect recipes for the baking contest. Sign-ups were the next day, and there was a form to fill out.

The Alden children lived with their grandfather. After their parents had died, they'd run away and hidden in a railroad boxcar in the woods. The children had heard that Grandfather Alden was mean. Even though they'd never met him, they were afraid. But when Grandfather finally found the children, they discovered he wasn't mean at all. Now the children lived in his house in Greenfield. Their boxcar was a clubhouse in the backyard.

In the boxcar, their wirehaired terrier, Watch, was waiting.

"Watch!" Benny was excited to tell the dog about the contest. "I'm going to be a sous-chef." Watch lay down on the floor as Benny explained what that meant. Then Benny whispered to Watch, "You can't help with baking because dogs can't bake. But I can sneak you some tasters if you want."

Watch barked happily.

"We need the right equipment." Jessie looked through a box of cooking supplies she had stored in a corner. "This isn't going to be like making snacks while we hang out." She pulled out some measuring cups and a big mixing bowl.

"The sign-up form is on the back of the flyer," Henry said as he grabbed a pencil. "You and Benny will have two rounds where you get to choose what to make and one round where the judges give you surprise ingredients, and you make what they say."

"Two original recipes," Jessie said. She told Benny, "Your first job as sous-chef is to help me think about what two recipes we are going to make."

"I like popcorn," Benny said as Jessie dug a cookbook out of the box. "And carrots with dip." He smiled and held up two fingers. "That should cover it. Easy-peasy!"

Jessie breathed a heavy sigh. "The recipes have to be desserts, remember? And those kinds of snacks don't use baking. Baking is special. It's about using heat, like in an oven, to make foods. We're going to need good recipes and the perfect ingredients. There's a lot of science involved to get everything to bake together just right." She opened her notebook and began to make a list of the dishes and tools she needed to get from Grandfather's kitchen. With every passing minute, Jessie was growing more and more nervous about the contest. She frowned and muttered, "This is very hard. So many things can go wrong. I could burn the dessert. Add too much salt. Or not enough salt. Or mess up the artistic decorations. Or..."

"You know what's also important in baking?" Benny asked Jessie.

She looked up at him.

A Contest

"A no-worrying, smiling face," he said.

Jessie shook her head. "You're right!" She relaxed and smiled. "No more stressing. This contest will be fun."

"I know what the first poster for our team should say." Violet grabbed her markers.

"What?" Henry asked.

Violet chuckled. "Benny's 'sous-chef' cheer inspired me to write a rhyme."

"I can't wait to hear it," Benny said. "*Moo* rhymes with *sous*. You can use that. Or *chef* rhymes with…" He thought about it. "Nothing very cheery. Clef? Ref? Hmmm."

"I have another idea." Violet quickly wrote the words on a big poster board then held up their newest cheer.

Everyone chanted the words together: "Bake it with a grin. That's how the Aldens win!"

CHAPTER 2

Signing Up

There was a line outside Greenfield Bakery. The main street through town had small shops and restaurants next to each other stretching for a few blocks, and the bakery was in the exact middle. It had been there since Grandfather Alden was a child, and a lot of the cakes and cookies were made with the same recipes from all those years ago.

The flyer said that the winners of this year's bake-off would get to choose one of their creations to add to the bakery menu.

"Oh dear. Are all these kids signing up for the contest?" Jessie wondered, pushing back a new wave of nerves. She looked at the line that stretched from the bakery past the hardware store next door.

Signing Up

Benny took Jessie's hand in his and squeezed it. "The more contestants, the more desserts there will be to taste!"

"Always thinking positively," Henry said, winking at Benny.

"Always thinking with my tummy," Benny replied with a grin.

"Hi, Jessie." A girl Jessie knew tapped her on the shoulder. Emma had dark hair braided tightly and pulled back with a purple ribbon. Jessie was used to how softly Emma always spoke. She leaned in to hear her.

"Are you signing up for the competition?" Emma asked.

"Yes. Looks like you are too." Jessie noticed the form in Emma's hand.

"My older brother wants to bake. I'm helping," Emma said with a frown.

"Are you the sous-chef?" Benny asked. "I am!" he announced proudly.

Emma said, "I suppose I'm Connor's sous-chef if that means I get to fill out the entry paperwork, wash the dishes, and clean up after him."

"That doesn't sound very fun to me," Benny said. "And not very sous-chef-y."

"It's what Connor told me to do." Emma shrugged. "I don't want to—" She didn't finish her thought because her brother interrupted.

"Hey, Sis!" Connor pointed to the bakery door. "Hurry up. It's our turn!"

"I gotta go," Emma told Benny with a frown. "Connor forgot the entry form at home. Part of my job was to run back to get it."

Violet noticed the beads of sweat on Emma's forehead. She whispered to Henry, "Emma doesn't seem happy to be in the contest."

"I thought that too," Henry agreed. Emma seemed so unenthusiastic compared to Benny, who was bouncing on his toes, impatient to get started.

"Tell me about the recipes again, Jessie," Benny said as they watched Emma and Connor turn in their entry form.

"We have to make three different desserts," Jessie explained for the hundredth time. "For the first one and the last one, we bring our own recipes. We can even practice baking them at home."

Signing Up

"I volunteer to make sure it's good!" Benny licked his lips. "But what about the second dessert? Can I sample that one too?"

"You can't because the second dessert is a mystery," Henry reminded Benny. "You'll get everything you need to make it when you get to the contest table."

"Aldens love mysteries, and dessert mysteries are the best kind of mystery." Benny clapped his hands.

"Let's focus on the recipes we need to bring," Jessie suggested. "I don't know what to make yet."

The line was moving quickly.

Violet started naming things that were baked in an oven. "Cookies. Cake. Muffins. Croissants."

"Cake pops. Cinnamon rolls," Henry added.

Benny sniffed the air. "I smell cinnamon-apple pie. We could make that." Benny quickly changed his mind. "Nah. We'd never make it as good as Mrs. Catalan's." Mrs. Catalan was the current owner of Greenfield Bakery. "Hers is the best." Benny sniffed the air again and asked, "Can we get some pie for a snack? It's hot out of the oven!"

"How do you know the pie is hot?" Violet asked.

"We're still outside the bakery, standing in line."

"My nose knows," Benny said. "And all this talk about food is making me hungry." He asked again, "Please?"

"Sure," Henry told him. "I'm a little hungry too. Violet and I will go buy the pieces of pie and get a table while you and Jessie register for the contest." As Henry and Violet went inside, Mrs. Catalan called, "Next!" It was Benny and Jessie's turn at the sign-up table.

Jessie handed Mrs. Catalan the entry form.

Mrs. Catalan took the form, wrote down their names on a lined piece of paper, then looked up. "Jessie Alden. Benny Alden." She smiled. "Two of my favorite customers." Mrs. Catalan wrote number ten on the top of their form. "You're the last ones in the competition. We can only have ten teams. Registration is now officially closed."

She handed them each a Greenfield Bakery apron and a piece of paper with the rules printed on it. "We will meet at the contest tables on Friday. There will be a big, white tent in the park—you can't miss it! Bring your ingredients list, and you'll get to see your baking station." She stopped Benny and Jessie before they walked away. "Read the rules carefully. The first recipe category has changed slightly. We've added an exciting twist." She winked. "Good luck!"

"Whew," Jessie said with a sigh of relief as she and Benny slipped into a booth with Henry and Violet. "We turned in our entry form just in time."

Benny looked toward the bakery door. They'd been the last in line, but now there was one girl, a few years older than Henry, leaning on Mrs. Catalan's contest sign-up table. She had red hair tied with a bright green ribbon.

"I want to sign up," she told Mrs. Catalan, who was packing up extra aprons and rule sheets.

The Aldens could hear their conversation.

"I'm sorry," Mrs. Catalan said. "The contest is full."

"But I need to be in the contest!" the girl said.

Mrs. Catalan shook her head. "I can't add any more teams. Sorry."

The girl bit her lip, turned sharply, and left the bakery.

A few minutes later, the door opened with a bang.

The Great Greenfield Bake-Off

"Mrs. Catalan!" a man's voice echoed through the bakery. "I need to talk to you."

"That's Steve Lin from The Bread Box," Jessie said. The Bread Box was a new bakery in Greenfield. It had only been open a few weeks.

"I think it's weird that he decided to open a bakery across the street from this bakery," Violet said. They'd talked about this before.

"Mr. Lin makes great cupcakes," Benny said. "But Mrs. Catalan makes the best pies."

"Still," Henry said, "it might have been smarter for him to set up his shop farther away."

"I like having two bakeries so close," Benny said, licking a bit of apple filling off his fingers. "I think every store on Main Street should be a bakery."

Henry smiled. He turned to see what Mr. Lin was upset about. But Mrs. Catalan and Mr. Lin had moved to a corner. "I just heard Mr. Lin complaining that his bakery isn't part of the bake-off competition. He seems really mad about being left out."

"That's the saddest thing I ever heard." Benny rubbed his eyes as if he was going to cry. "Bakers

shouldn't fight. They should be friends and make beautiful cakes together." He went on. "Vanilla cakes with chocolate frosting and rainbow sprinkles."

"Those two are definitely *not* planning to bake a friendship cake," Violet said, watching as Mr. Lin stormed out of the bakery, slamming the door behind him.

"Who would argue about something as wonderful as a bake-off?" Benny asked. He finished the last bit of his pie in one big bite. "That would be very silly."

Through the window, Jessie could see Mr. Lin clomping angrily across the street to his own bakery shop. Goosebumps skittered up her arms. Jessie had a bad feeling about the argument they'd just heard. She decided to put it out of her mind. Benny was probably right. No one would argue about a bake-off, right? That really would be silly.

Something Strange

Friday afternoon, Jessie, Benny, Violet, and Henry went to visit the park where the Great Greenfield Bake-Off competition was going to be held.

Watch loved going to the park. He bounded along happily next to Violet, who held his leash.

Jessie held the list of ingredients for their recipes tightly in her hand. That piece of paper was precious, and she didn't want to drop it by accident!

"Whoa!" Benny's eyes widened as they walked across the lawn. The contest was set up near the playground, at almost the same spot where they'd been when Benny got the flyer for the competition. Only now the grass was covered by a large wooden floor and a huge, white, pop-up tent.

The Great Greenfield Bake-Off

The Aldens tied Watch's leash to a shady tree near the tent and went inside to look around.

There were ten tables made into workstations that faced a long tasting table where the judges would sit. Each station had a counter with a mixing bowl in the center. A sink was off to the side. Beneath each counter was an oven. And behind the work areas, there were several small refrigerators, one for each team.

"It's like they moved the best parts of Grandfather's kitchen here!" Jessie was impressed. In each station's cupboards were pots and pans and baking dishes. "I don't have to bring anything from home," she added. "Mrs. Catalan has really invested a lot into this competition."

"Whoa," Benny repeated. "This is amazing. The only thing better would be if the fridge were full of snacks!" He opened one of the refrigerators and peeked inside. "Sad. It's empty."

"We're going to fill ours with our own creations," Jessie said, still clutching her list, hoping they'd chosen impressive desserts that were both tasty and nice to look at. Presentation was a big part of a team's score. The food had to be delicious plus creative and pretty. Violet had really helped Jessie and Benny with the artistic part of their recipes.

"There are viewing stands right here." Henry pointed to a nearby area where stadium seats were set up, facing the kitchen workspaces. "They're so close, we'll be able to see everything that happens. Violet and I will get Watch and pick out the best seats." Henry gave Benny a high-five. "We'll meet you when you're done for the day."

"This shouldn't take very long," Jessie said. "Today we're just turning in our list of ingredients and getting the rules. It'll be quick."

"I hope they tell us which station will be our own little baking spot," Benny added. "That's where the yummy magic is going to happen." He rubbed his belly. "Oh, look! There's Mrs. Catalan. Maybe she brought snacks?" They all turned to see Mrs. Catalan unloading pastry boxes from the Greenfield Bakery van. "I smell chocolate," Benny said happily. "With salt and almonds."

Jessie didn't smell anything. "Come on, Benny," she said. "Bring your talented nose. The other contestants are gathering by that banner." They headed over.

There was a big banner in rainbow colors announcing the competition. Benny and Jessie immediately noticed Connor and Emma in the center of the group. Since they didn't know anyone else, they decided to say hi.

"Hey Emma," Benny said. "Did you bring your ingredients list? Did you find some great recipes?"

"We—" Emma began, but Connor interrupted her.

"Don't tell them anything, Sis. They're the competition!" He turned to Jessie, "This is your assistant?" He tipped his head toward Benny. "Isn't he too young for something so important? He might mess everything up."

"There wasn't an age requirement," Jessie said, feeling like she needed to defend Benny.

Benny didn't need defending. He puffed out his chest and announced, "I'm a very good sous-chef." He corrected himself, saying, "Not that I've ever been one before, but I plan to be the best one here."

"I'm the top chef," Connor said. "My recipe is going to win and be on the menu at Greenfield

Bakery. Emma's just my helper."

Jessie noticed Emma pinch her lips, like she had something to say but decided against it.

"Benny's more than a helper," Jessie said. "We're a team."

"Team Alden," Benny said proudly.

"Well then," Connor announced. "It's Team Alden versus Connor Green."

"And Emma Green," Benny put in, but Connor didn't seem to hear.

"Good luck to you," Connor said to Jessie as Mrs. Catalan told the contestants to make a line to hand in their ingredients lists. "May the best baker win." He grabbed Emma's hand and tugged her away, rushing to be first in the line.

"Emma is nice," Jessie said, as they stood patiently in line with the other teams. "But I wonder why she's doing the contest with her brother when he's so bossy."

"He really, really, really wants to win, doesn't he?" Benny said. "I think he's forgetting the fun part." He put out his pinky to Jessie for a pinky promise. "Bake it with a grin?"

The Great Greenfield Bake-Off

Jessie linked pinkies with Benny and shook. She finished the cheer. "That's how the Aldens win."

Benny watched Emma and Connor finish in line and walk into the tent to pick out their workstation. "And even if we don't win, we still grin?"

Jessie shook Benny's pinky again. "Definitely." She gave him a sample of the world's biggest grin.

They turned in their ingredients list and were told to go into the tent to pick a station. Jessie led Benny to one as far away from Connor and Emma as possible. She wanted to be able to focus on her own baking without wondering what Connor was doing. If they were going to have fun and make great desserts, Jessie didn't want any distractions.

She checked that the oven heated up, that the fridge was cold, then took a good look at the pots and pans provided. Everything was wonderful! "This is going to be so fun," she gushed to Benny. "I'm glad you got that flyer."

"Me too!" Benny smiled.

"Welcome, welcome, welcome." Mrs. Catalan stood at the front of the workspace. "I am so excited to be hosting the Great Greenfield Bake-Off. The competition, as you know, starts tomorrow. I looked at your ingredients lists and look forward to tasting your dishes." She reminded them that pretty presentation was important. "I hope everyone read the rules carefully. Tomorrow's first dessert has a twist, I mean, a twist for a bake-off." She grinned. "There will be no baking in your first dessert recipe! It's the no-bake bake-off."

The kids at the workstations all laughed except Benny.

Everyone had known about the no-bake plan for the bake-off since the day they turned in the entry form. And every few hours, every day since, Benny had complained how it didn't make sense.

"No-bake baking is confusing," Benny said.

Jessie then noticed Emma hadn't laughed at Mrs. Catalan's no-bake baking joke either. She was staring at the audience bleachers, not really paying attention.

"I am one of three judges," Mrs. Catalan continued, looking serious. "Tomorrow, you'll meet the other judges." She motioned toward someone near her van. Jessie couldn't see who was there.

The Great Greenfield Bake-Off

"Starting now, if you need anything or have questions, please see the bake-off contest assistant, Leslie Smallwater."

A familiar girl with bright-red hair stepped out from behind the bakery van. She was carrying a clipboard.

"Isn't that the girl who wanted to sign up but couldn't?" Benny asked Jessie.

"Yes. She was too late to get her entry in." Jessie watched the girl whisper something to Mrs. Catalan before moving alone to the front of the tent. "Looks like she's the contest assistant now."

"I wonder if she gets to taste all of the desserts like a judge?" Benny asked. "That would be an excellent job!"

"I don't know what she does," said Jessie.

Leslie explained. "Hi all. I am going to review the rules. Please pay careful attention." Her voice sounded tired.

Jessie had a notebook with her. She wanted to write everything down so she wouldn't forget. She glanced around the tent. Almost every team had someone writing notes as well. Emma had a notebook, and Connor pointed at a blank page.

"Tomorrow, there will be two rounds," Leslie said in that same low, sleepy voice. She didn't look up from the clipboard. "When you arrive in the morning, you'll find all the ingredients you need

for your first recipe." She added, "I'm shopping from the list you gave us, so if something is missing, it's not my fault."

The Great Greenfield Bake-Off

Jessie mentally reviewed her ingredients list to make sure she wrote down everything she needed. Violet had double checked her list. Henry had triple checked it. She felt sure the list was good.

"The second round tomorrow will be after a lunch break. It's the mystery round. The judges will give you the ingredients and recipe for what you will make. Not everyone will make it through these two rounds." She kept her eyes glued to the clipboard and said, without any emotion, "Some of you will go home."

Benny grabbed Jessie's hand and squeezed it. He whispered, "Not us. Don't let it be us."

Leslie quickly checked her watch, then said, "For the remaining contestants, Sunday is the grand finale. Your desserts will be judged on taste, presentation, and creativity." Lowering her clipboard, Leslie finally looked around the tent. "Any questions?"

Benny's hand shot up. "Are there treats today?"

"No." Leslie turned away from him. "Other questions?"

Benny's hand shot up again. Leslie called on

him a second time.

"Can we taste the desserts the other teams make?"

"Yes." With that simple answer, she dismissed everyone. "See you all tomorrow." Leslie walked quickly away.

Jessie watched Leslie leave. It had seemed like she really wanted to be in the competition the other day, but now Leslie acted like she didn't want to be there. Jessie wondered what changed. Maybe she was just tired.

"Tomorrow's going to be the best day!" Benny cheered. "Today would have been the best day, but there weren't any snacks. So tomorrow will have to be the best."

"We might be on TV!" A boy from the team at the table next to Benny and Jessie showed them where the local news crew was setting up their cameras.

"I've never been on TV before," a different boy from a workstation near the back of the tent said.

Everyone gathered around to talk about the TV crew.

"I've been on television many times," Connor announced. "It's not a big deal."

The Great Greenfield Bake-Off

"I am going to call my mom," a girl said. "I feel like a celebrity already."

The conversation turned to recipes and ingredients. Since they'd already turned in their shopping lists and couldn't change what they'd chosen to make, everyone was willing to share what they were baking. But not Connor. He told Emma, "It's time to go. I want to practice my recipe one more time at home before I make it for the judges tomorrow." Emma nodded and they quickly left.

Henry and Violet came to find Benny and Jessie. Watch loved all the commotion and greeted everyone.

Benny introduced Henry and Violet to the other contestants, since now they were becoming friends. Henry already knew one girl, named Melanie, from a book club he'd gone to at the library. Violet knew a team of twin boys from her art class. Most of the other kids were new to them, but everyone chatted away because they all loved to bake.

As they were leaving, Henry told Jessie and Benny what they'd witnessed while sitting in the audience.

Something Strange

"While you were going over the rules, we saw something strange," Henry said.

Violet nodded.

"After Mrs. Catalan left Leslie to talk to you, she went to talk to a man hanging more bake-off banners," Henry said.

"We heard them talking. Tomorrow, there will be numbers hanging above each workstation," Violet said. "You're at number three."

"Lucky three," Benny echoed. He clapped his hands. Watch lay down by Benny's feet to rest.

"What's strange about that?" asked Jessie.

"Mrs. Catalan was angry that they weren't up already. It sounded like someone else had told the man not to hang the numbers. Mrs. Catalan told him not to talk to anyone except her." Henry glanced over to where the Greenfield Bakery van had been parked. It was gone now. "I've never seen Mrs. Catalan so upset before."

"That is strange," said Jessie. "Mrs. Catalan has everything with the bake-off planned out so well. It's not like her for there to be a mix-up."

"I think there's something else weird going on,"

The Great Greenfield Bake-Off

Violet told them all. She pointed to where a man was standing in a shadowy place by the audience stands. It was obvious that the man was trying not to be noticed. Anytime anyone got close, he ducked farther into the shadows. Violet only noticed him because of where she was standing. If she'd been just an inch to the right, she wouldn't have seen him at all. "That looks like Mr. Lin. Doesn't it?" She moved over so her siblings could see what she saw.

"What could he be doing here?" Jessie wondered. "His bakery is not involved in the competition, and the other day he seemed to be arguing with Mrs. Catalan."

When Violet looked again, Mr. Lin was gone.

"Hmm," Henry said, rubbing his chin. "We better pay extra attention tomorrow. If there's something strange going on at the bake-off, the Aldens will figure it out."

CHAPTER 4

The Contest Begins

"Welcome to the Great Greenfield Bake-Off!"

Jessie noted that Leslie Smallwater sounded more energetic now than she had the day before. "I think Leslie got a good night's sleep," she told Benny.

The tent was bustling with activity. The camera crew was there, ready to film the events for the evening news. The stands for the audience were packed. There were probably a hundred people watching, maybe more. Plus, all the people who would see the event on TV. Mrs. Catalan was all dressed up, smiling for the cameras and the audience. She looked excited for the competition to start. Jessie's heart was racing. This was huge.

Violet had made signs to cheer on Jessie and

Benny. Other people had signs to support their bakers too. Some people held balloons. There was excitement in the air.

The weather was perfect, not too hot and not too cold. It was a great day for baking.

Jessie and Benny greeted the other contestants as they made their way to their station. Everyone was animated and obviously nervous. Except for Connor and Emma. They weren't greeting anyone. They stood at their kitchen station, still and ready, staring at Leslie for instructions to begin.

Jessie and Benny were wearing their bake-off aprons. They went to stand behind their baking station. Everyone was told they had to keep their hands firmly against their sides until they heard the opening bell. Then they had two hours to complete their desserts and present them for judging.

"I know you explained it to me a lot of times, but it's still no-bake-baffling. Tell me *again* why we are not baking for the bake-off?" Benny asked Jessie after Leslie explained the rules to the audience.

"This is the big twist Mrs. Catalan was talking

about," Jessie said. "Normally baking requires heat. But there are some desserts that are exactly like baked desserts that don't require time in an oven or any heat at all."

Since he couldn't move his arms, Benny raised his shoulders and tilted his head. "Makes no sense," he told her.

"Stop thinking about it or you'll get a headache," Jessie told him. "Let's just bake! All the ingredients for our no-bake chocolate lasagna are here, and we are ready to make it."

"But not bake it," Benny put in with one last shrug.

"Exactly," Jessie said with a giggle. "Now you've got it."

She glanced over the ingredients on their worktable. She checked each one off in her head. The crust was made of chocolate wafer cookies and butter. Cooking spray kept it from sticking to the dish.

Cream cheese, sugar, milk, vanilla, and whipping cream for the first layer.

The next layer was chocolate pudding mix and more milk.

The Great Greenfield Bake-Off

Jessie double checked that there was enough milk for everything they'd put it in. They had a half-gallon carton. That was plenty.

The recipe called for a topping of chocolate chips and more whipped cream, but creativity was a big part of the score. Presentation was too, so Jessie and Benny had decided that since regular lasagna was an Italian food, they'd decorate the top of their dessert in honor of the Italian flag. The flag was green, white, and red. They'd have a thick stripe of green grapes, a stripe of mini marshmallows and a stripe of cut strawberries.

All those ingredients had been on the list.

Jessie felt relieved that everything they needed was there. The sugar was in a clear jar with a handwritten label. All the other stuff was in original containers from the store. Jessie noticed that the worktables around her also had sugar in bins. That made sense because everyone was using a lot of sugar, so they probably brought one big bag from the bakery and divided it up. Her brain measured what she'd need. They'd have extra.

"Ready?" she asked Benny as Leslie finished

talking to the audience.

"I am, but I don't think Connor is," Benny said, glancing in Connor's direction. Connor was wearing a tall, white, puffy chef's hat. Like them, his hands were stuck to his sides as he waited to start.

"That hat is so fancy," Jessie said. "He looks like a professional chef."

"Yep, his hat is cool," Benny replied. "But Emma is missing."

"Oh," Jessie said. She hadn't noticed that Connor was standing alone. "I guess I thought she was blocked by the hat."

"Here she comes," Benny said, noticing that Emma was dashing in from behind the audience stands. She was breathing hard as she took her position next to her brother. She looked worried.

"I am getting the idea that Emma really doesn't want to do this contest," Jessie remarked. "She looks so scared!"

"I'm scared too," Benny said. "I don't want to mess up."

"It's going to be great," Jessie said. "No matter what happens, we are going to do our best."

Suddenly Leslie was standing by their station. "Hey," she whispered. "Have you seen my clipboard?"

"Is it missing?" Benny asked. "We're extra-special good at finding lost things."

"I must have just put it somewhere and forgot," Leslie moaned. "Don't tell anyone. I just thought maybe you'd seen it around this workstation."

"I don't think it's here," Jessie said. "We'll let you know if we see it."

"Thanks," Leslie sighed. "On with the show, I suppose." She dashed back to the front of the bake-off. "Bakers!" Leslie called. "On the count of three, everyone can begin." She started the countdown. "One, two..."

Violet called out to Jessie and Benny from the stands, "Bake it with a grin."

"That's how the Aldens win!" Henry finished.

"Three!" A bell rang. The timer started. The bake-off had begun.

Jessie and Benny had agreed on a system. She'd measure; he'd mix.

There was a mixing bowl provided for them. And a glass dish to layer their ingredients in. The refrigerator was the most important thing for them to get their chocolate lasagna done on time.

"Don't forget, Benny," Jessie said. "Normally, the recipe says it takes three hours to chill. We don't have that much time today."

"I remember," Benny said. "We'll use the freezer. It's colder." He wrapped his arms around himself and said, "Brrrr." Then he added, "Can I lick the spoon?"

Jessie snorted. "No time for licking."

"There's always time for licking," Benny said. "But I'll be patient." He raised his mixing spoon. "No-Bake Baker Benny is ready!"

Jessie put chocolate wafer cookies in a plastic bag and handed it to Benny.

"I am pretending that I am a superhero called De Crusher," he announced, flexing a muscle. "My power is to smash stuff." He began smashing the cookies into crumbles with the back of the mixing spoon. "Take that, yummy cookie! You'll never escape my mighty strength!"

While Benny squished and squashed the cookies to bitty bits, Jessie melted some butter on the small kitchen stove. They combined the crumbs and the melted butter in a mixing bowl, and Benny stirred it all up. Jessie pressed the crust into the oil-sprayed pan.

Jessie measured the sugar and put it into another bowl. It didn't look like the same sugar they had at Grandfather's house. "I'm sure it's sweet and delicious," she muttered as she moved on to measuring the cream cheese.

When the first layer was ready, she layered the sugary cream cheese on top of the crust.

"I think I should lick the spoon," Benny suggested.

"No time." Jessie shook her head. "Off to the freezer!"

Benny grabbed the dish and dashed away.

At the refrigerators, he ran into Emma, who was about to place her team's dish into their freezer.

"Having fun?" Benny asked.

"Fun?" Emma seemed confused by the question. She was trying to balance a pan of cheesecake mix and open the freezer door at the same time.

Benny reached over to help her. That was when Emma dropped a plastic baggie that had been

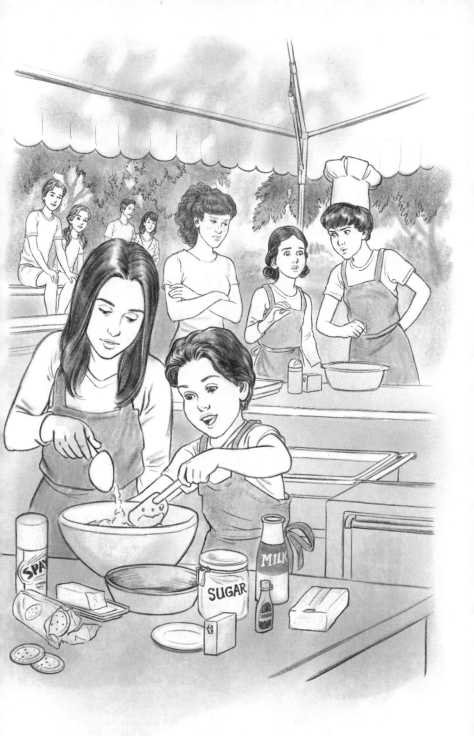

tucked under her cheesecake. She quickly thrust the cake in the freezer and snagged the baggie off the floor. Benny noticed the baggie didn't look like what Leslie had put their ingredients in.

Emma pretended nothing strange happened. And before Benny could ask her about it, Connor shouted, "Hurry up! We're running behind."

Emma stuffed the baggie, which was filled with something brown with white speckles, in the pocket of her apron and muttered, "Thanks, Benny," then hurried away.

Benny went back to his station. "I think maybe Emma and Connor snuck in an extra ingredient," he told Jessie. "But I'm not sure." He told her what he'd seen.

Jessie didn't know what to make of it. "Let's tell Henry and Violet to watch them closely in the next round," she suggested. "We have to stay focused and finish our own dessert in time."

Soon the chocolate pudding layer was ready. Benny got the dessert from the freezer, they layered the pudding on top of the cream cheese, and knowing Jessie's answer, he asked, "Can I lick

The Contest Begins

the spoon?"

She laughed and pointed to the freezer. "No time. Go."

Benny carried the dessert.

"Twenty minutes!" Leslie announced. "You should be decorating your dessert now."

Benny and Jessie were ready. Jessie had already cut the fruit toppings and put the mini marshmallows in a bowl. But across the room, they could hear Connor arguing with Emma. It was clear they weren't prepared. Neither were the two boys at another table. Something had gone wrong with the boys' dessert, and it was warm and soupy, not chilled and firm. They were laughing at what a mess their dessert turned out to be. A team near the back of the room was finished. They were playing cards while they waited for the judging.

Jessie placed the last strawberry in the Italian flag when Leslie blew a horn. "Time's up," she said. "Place your desserts at the end of your tables and step away."

Music played as the judges arrived.

The Great Greenfield Bake-Off

"That's Daniel Prince," Jessie told Benny, noting the judge behind Mrs. Catalan. "He is a food critic on TV."

"What's a food critic?" Benny asked.

"Someone who tastes food then talks about why it's good or bad," Jessie explained.

"That's a job?" Benny clapped his hands. "How come I didn't know that? He gets paid to eat— that's genius!" Benny was very impressed with Daniel Prince, until the next judge stepped into the tent.

"That's Merry Holiday!" said Benny. "I watch her TV show all the time. She shops."

"For what?" Jessie asked. She thought Merry Holiday sounded like a made-up name.

"*Food*," Benny said as if it were obvious. "Snacks and healthy food for people who need help getting stuff." He added, "It's a kids' show. She's very nice."

"I hope she's nice to us," Jessie said.

"Merry Holiday is nice to everyone," Benny told her.

The contestants waited while the three judges

walked around the workstations. They looked at each dessert, making notes on appearance, while Leslie cut slices to take back to the judging table.

The winner of the round would be announced when everyone returned to the tent from the lunch break.

"Can I lick the spoon now?" Benny asked.

"YES!" Jessie handed him a clean spoon.

Benny eagerly dipped the spoon into the leftover chocolate lasagna, taking a big heaping bite. Then he spit it right back out.

"Gross!" he gagged.

"Gross?" Jessie grabbed another spoon and took her own taste. "Salt!" she declared. "How did that happen?" She stared at their pretty dessert that was terrible to taste. "There isn't even salt in the recipe! This is all wrong." Jessie put her head in her hands. "There's no way we're going to win this round."

CHAPTER

It's a Mystery

Mrs. McGregor, the housekeeper at Grandfather's, had packed sandwiches for them. Jessie and Benny chose a grassy spot near the tent to have their lunch. Henry and Violet joined them.

"I'm starving," Benny said, opening his paper bag and peeking inside. "Oh, turkey with cranberry sauce and mayonnaise and extra ketchup!" He dug the sandwich out of the bag.

Jessie heard a group nearby talking about their dessert. They were talking loudly, so it was easy to hear what they were saying. Henry, Violet, and Benny heard them too.

A boy with brown hair was telling a blond girl, "We were so busy we didn't taste our dessert until after the judges left. When we finally got a bite, it tasted terrible. I don't understand what happened," he said.

They were clearly on different teams. The girl shrugged. "Maybe you could have fixed the problem if you'd tasted your dessert all along?"

The boy said, "I just don't get it. I followed the directions exactly. Our chocolate mud pie was perfect at home."

The girl shrugged again. "We should be sure to check every ingredient in the next round."

The boy agreed. The conversation faded to a whisper as they moved away.

"Sounds like they had problems too," Benny told Jessie, looking back at the other team.

"I wonder if anyone else had issues with their dessert," Violet said.

Benny saw Emma and Connor nearby. He decided to ask them. He went over to their blanket. "Did you taste your dessert before the judges took some?"

"We tasted everything." Connor licked his lips and said, "My dessert was perfect."

"Why are you asking?" Emma wanted to know.

"It's just that—" Benny began when Connor interrupted.

"Shhh, Emma," Connor said quickly. "Focus on lunch. We need to eat fast and get ready for round two."

Emma had that look again, like she wanted to say something to her brother, but didn't.

Benny went back to his lunch spot. "Connor and Emma didn't have a problem with their ingredients. So, it didn't happen to everyone," he reported.

Henry glanced over to the judges' table. "They must still be on their lunch break."

"We have something else to tell you," Benny told Henry and Violet.

"We think Connor and Emma might have brought in outside ingredients." Jessie explained that Benny had seen Emma with a baggie. Then she took a big bite of her sandwich. They needed to get back to the tent soon.

"Maybe Connor forgot something he needed?" Violet unwrapped her sandwich. She hadn't started eating yet.

The Great Greenfield Bake-Off

"It would be against the rules to bring your own ingredients," Henry reminded everyone. He glanced over at Connor and Emma. Connor was talking. Emma was listening and nodding. "He really wants to win, but I don't know if he'd cheat to get his dessert on the menu at the bakery."

"Cheating isn't fun," Benny said, getting a cookie from his bag. "This is supposed to be a fun day." He began to unwrap the cookie, then Jessie stopped him.

"Benny, can you save that for later?" she asked. "Don't get too full."

"This is my first dessert today," Benny said. "Since tasting our gross lasagna doesn't count—" he opened his mouth wide for a bite.

"Wait!" Jessie put up a hand. "I changed my mind about something important."

Benny raised his eyebrows and held the cookie in midair.

"There's always time for licking the spoon," she said.

"I tried to tell you that," Benny grinned. Then he realized what she meant. "Oh. I get it. We're going to make sure everything tastes right, right?"

"Exactly." Jessie packed up her own lunch cookie. "This round, I want you to taste everything as we go."

"Good idea," he agreed. "So, I need to keep an empty space in my tummy for dessert testing." Benny handed his cookie to Violet. "Good-bye, dear cookie friend. I'll eat you later." Benny looked down at his tummy. "This spot, right by my belly button, will be the tasting spot. It'll fill up with the surprise dessert that we are about to make."

A bell rang. It was time for the chefs to return to the kitchen.

"We'll watch for anything unusual," Henry told Jessie and Benny. They threw out their trash.

"And anyone acting strange," Violet added.

"Thanks!" Jessie said.

"Bake it with a grin," Benny said this time.

"That's how the Aldens win!" Henry said, then he and Violet hurried to their seats in the audience.

Leslie met the contestants in the kitchen.

Merry Holiday, Daniel Prince, and Mrs. Catalan were seated around a long table where the teams' desserts were displayed. They each had a spoon in one hand and a pencil in the other.

Leslie Smallwater was standing near the judges with her clipboard.

"She found it." Jessie pointed out the clipboard to Benny.

"Without us?" he giggled. "How?"

"You think we're the only ones who can solve mysteries?" Jessie giggled back at him.

"Well—" Benny began, but stopped when the judging began.

All three judges took big bites of Team Four's peanut butter pudding at the same time. Then they all three spit out the dessert onto the table. Daniel Prince was coughing. Merry Holiday was gagging. Mrs. Catalan asked for water.

Leslie rushed to the closest sink and filled three glasses.

"Looks like another dessert was ruined," Jessie told Benny.

"This is bad," Benny said, watching as the judges went on to spit out a caramel shortbread pie. "Very, very bad."

It's a Mystery

The judges didn't give up. Their bites got a lot smaller, but still, they tasted all the desserts, spitting and gagging and drinking big glasses of water as they went.

It came time for Benny and Jessie's chocolate lasagna.

Even though Benny had tasted their dessert, he hoped that somehow the slices the judges were sampling would be different. But when each of them took a bite, they each had the same reaction. They immediately spit it all back out, then they guzzled water.

The only dessert that the judges ate happily was Connor and Emma's no-bake pumpkin cheesecake.

Finally, Leslie declared that it was time to announce the winner of the first round. First she explained for the audience and TV cameras, "There was a problem with some ingredients for most of our teams," she said. "Somehow salt and sugar were switched in every dessert except one."

There was a gasp from the viewing stands and cries of "Oh no!"

Jessie noticed Mrs. Catalan didn't look excited

anymore—she looked upset. She worked so hard on the competition and having a big mix-up in round one wasn't good.

Leslie went on, tapping her pencil on the clipboard. "The judges have decided that the one team that didn't have an ingredient mix-up gets first place." She didn't even say the team name before Connor began to cheer.

The audience applauded. Emma gave half a smile. And one person in the audience clapped and hooted, "Congratulations! Way to go! Yay!"

Jessie looked to see who was cheering so eagerly.

"It's Mr. Lin!" Benny announced. He'd looked toward the loud voice too. "I wonder what he's doing here?"

"Supporting Connor and Emma, I suppose," Jessie said. "Maybe he knows them?"

Mr. Lin gave one more holler then slipped out of the audience stands and walked away.

The TV crew gathered around Connor and Emma at their workstation. Connor straightened his chef's hat. Emma was pushed aside by Connor as the reporter began to ask him questions about the pumpkin cheesecake recipe.

Leslie hurried over to Benny and Jessie. She said softly, "Your dessert was in first place for presentation and creativity. Too bad about the salt. Better luck in round two." She hurried off before Jessie or Benny could ask any questions.

Leslie was at the judging table. She had a microphone. "Round two begins in five minutes! Bakers, get ready for your surprise recipe!"

Round Two

"When I tell you to start, all bakers can look into the boxes on your stations," Leslie informed the contestants. "We've provided a recipe and all the ingredients you need for this round."

Benny leaned in toward Jessie. "I think I see a clue to the ingredient-switching mystery." He pointed to Leslie. "There's something white all over her shirt," Benny noted. "It's also all over the back of the clipboard."

Jessie squinted. "Good eyes."

"Good at tasting. Good at smelling. Good at seeing," Benny said. "Me and Watch have a lot in common."

Jessie wished they could get closer. "It could

be salt."

"Might be. Or sugar," Benny said. "Or flour."

Jessie said, "She's in charge of the ingredients, so maybe she set down her clipboard in something, and when she picked it up again, she got it on her shirt. It probably happened when she put everything on our workstations. Maybe it's not a clue to our mystery at all."

"But how did she know it was salt that had been switched in the desserts?" Benny asked.

"What do you mean?" Jessie said.

"Leslie told everyone salt had been switched for sugar when she said who won the first round," Benny said. "How did she know that?"

"I bet the judges tasted the salt in the desserts like we did in ours," Jessie told him. "Since salt and sugar look similar, it makes sense that that's where the mix-up happened."

"Hmm," said Benny. "I think we should tell Henry and Violet after the next round." When Jessie agreed, he added, "Now, please explain to me again, Jessie, why are we all making the exact same thing this contest round?"

The Great Greenfield Bake-Off

"To show how well we can follow directions," Jessie replied.

Benny nodded. "I'm a great rule follower. This time, we'll win for sure."

"I hope so," Jessie said, crossing her fingers. They had to make up for a disastrous first round.

"Bakers, ready?" Leslie asked.

"You know it!" Connor shouted. His loud voice filled the room. "After I win this round, my masterpiece will be on the menu!" He straightened his tall hat. "Forever."

Emma caught Benny's eye. She blushed and shrugged, with an expression like, "He's my brother. What can I do?"

Benny gave her a small smile and focused on their box.

"Bakers, bake!" Leslie rang a bell and the second round of competition began. "You have one hour."

"Graham crackers, butter, sugar." Benny was announcing each item as he pulled it from the box. "Salt." He set that one to the side. "We'll just use a wee bit this time."

"Here's the recipe," Jessie said, taking the note

card that was taped to the outside of the box. "S'mores cupcakes."

"Oh, so yummy!" Benny exclaimed. "I hope we win, and Mrs. Catalan will put them on the bakery menu!"

"Let's do our best," Jessie told him as she turned on the oven. "We need to get these in the oven as quickly as possible so they have time to cool before the judging."

Benny hurried to get the other ingredients on the counter. He was moving and talking fast. "Chocolate chips, heavy cream," he noted, "which isn't named correctly. It's actually very light to carry."

Jessie laughed as she poured the graham crackers into a mixing bowl and got started.

"We used marshmallows in the lasagna too," Benny said, as he set a bag next to the cream. "Good thing I love them!"

The cake called for flour, baking soda, baking powder, a pinch of salt, some of the sugar, cocoa powder, eggs, vanilla, and milk. Benny set those ingredients together and then set the big box on the floor. He looked at all the things they needed, spread across their work space. "It's easier to buy cupcakes than to make them," Benny said.

"I like baking," Jessie said while she poured melted butter, some sugar, and a touch of salt into the bowl with the graham crackers.

"I prefer eating," Benny said. "But if baking leads to eating, then it's all right by me!"

Jessie pushed the mixing bowl toward Benny. "First, tasting. Will you make sure the crust is sweet and not too salty?"

Benny took a quick pinch. "Just right," he said after testing it.

"Great." Jessie felt confident. She gave him some paper cupcake liners and a cupcake pan with twelve round spaces. "Please put the liners in the pan, then press some crust into each cupcake liner."

"Forty-five minutes remaining," Leslie warned. She was wandering around the room, checking on the teams and making notes on her clipboard.

Jessie scanned the recipe. Baking was going to take about sixteen minutes. Then they had to load the top with the chocolate and marshmallow mix and put the cupcakes back in the oven for about five more minutes. "We're on schedule," she told Benny. "But there's no room for any mistakes."

"Crusts are done," Benny reported. "What's next?"

Jessie checked the oven temperature. The contestants weren't allowed to put their cupcakes in or take them out themselves. It was Leslie's job so no one got burned by accident.

"Leslie!" Connor shouted her name. "Open the oven."

"How can they be cooking already?" Jessie asked Benny. "We still haven't mixed the batter." She checked around the room. It looked like everyone else was working on the batter. "I don't understand!"

"Maybe Emma is a superfast mixer," Benny suggested.

"I guess..." Jessie said, but in her heart she knew something was strange about how quickly Connor and Emma were getting through the recipe. She mixed up the cake batter as fast as she could, while being very careful to measure the ingredients correctly. When that was done, she told Benny, "Spoon the batter on top of the crust." Then she added, "Please."

"Taste it too?" Benny asked.

"You really shouldn't taste anything with raw egg in it," Jessie told him. "We'll have to trust it's okay."

"I'll use my other super senses," Benny told her. He tipped his ear to the bowl. "Sounds delicious." He sniffed the batter. "Smells perfect." He touched a bit of batter from the side of the bowl. "Texture is smooth as silk." Benny declared, "This cupcake batter is the best cupcake batter in Greenfield."

"All that without using your mouth?" Jessie asked. "Are you sure? We can't be too careful."

Benny gave a thumbs-up. "These cupcakes will be 1,000 percent yummy." He spooned scoops of batter on top of the graham cracker crusts.

"Leslie!" Jessie called. She glanced at the clock. They couldn't waste any time. "Open the oven, please."

Leslie hurried over. The oven was set to 350 degrees. As Leslie slipped the cupcake pan into the oven, Jessie put sixteen minutes on a timer.

"Can I go to the bathroom?" Emma called over to Leslie just as Leslie closed Jessie's oven. The rules said the bakers had to ask.

Leslie gave Emma permission, saying, "Come right back."

Jessie made the mistake of looking toward Connor while his sister walked away. Connor stuck out his tongue at Jessie.

"He's a strange guy," Jessie said under her breath.

The cupcakes were baking. It was time to mix the chocolate with the cream. "We're making a ganache," Jessie told Benny. "It's made out of two liquids that don't normally mix well. Oil and water usually stay apart, but we're going to use heat to force them to blend together."

"I never knew that baking was so much science." Benny sat down on the floor to watch the cupcakes bake. He stared at them through the small oven window. They needed to be soft on top, not totally cooked. The ganache would go on top, and then the cupcakes had to bake a little more.

Round Two

"Good thing I love science," Jessie said.

Benny decided that since the cupcakes were guaranteed to taste great, presentation was the next most important thing. "Bake, bake, bake little pretties," he said. "You are the most adorable cupcakes in the whole tent. No one is as adorable as you."

Jessie put a saucepan on a burner. The cool chocolate chips needed to melt and blend when the hot cream was poured on them. She was being careful, watching the time and making sure the cream didn't burn, when suddenly—the lights went out! The sunlight streaming into the tent was enough that they could all still see.

The boys at the station next to Jessie and Benny shouted, "The oven's off!"

A girl at the back yelled, "The stove went off too. My ganache is ruined!"

Another boy cried, "What will happen to the cupcakes?"

"What is going on, Jessie?" Benny looked up at his sister. He was still sitting on the floor. He said, "Salt instead of sugar this morning. Now the power goes out? The cupcakes aren't done yet. This is not good."

Jessie sighed. There was only one clear answer. "Someone is trying to ruin the bake-off."

CHAPTER 7

Trouble in the Tent

"How can we help?" Henry asked Leslie. He and Violet had come down from the audience as quickly as they could after the power went out.

"I..." She looked around the kitchen area frantically. Some of the teams' cupcakes never went into the oven. Others, like Connor and Emma's, were on the last few minutes of their first bake. "I don't know what to do," she admitted to him.

"I'll take a look at the breakers," Henry said. Those were the main electrical switches. They would usually be in a box, together, somewhere nearby.

"I'll help Henry," Violet said. She asked Leslie, "Any chance you know where those are?"

Leslie shook her head, as if trying to clear her

thoughts. "Maybe over there?" She pointed around the side of the kitchen area.

"What should we do?" Benny asked Jessie as Leslie dashed away in the opposite direction from Henry and Violet.

"I think we need to stay here." Jessie pointed at their oven. "The heat will keep baking the cupcakes as long as we keep the door closed. Maybe Henry will get the power back on quick enough that the temperature won't drop too much."

"I'll watch the cupcakes," Benny promised. "My adorable, little friends," he whispered through the oven door, "keep on baking and be extra beautiful, okay?"

Jessie tossed out the ruined warm cream. She'd need to start again once the power came back on.

As she put the cream in the garbage, she noticed Emma running back into the tent.

All around them, the teams were trying to decide what to do. No one wanted to toss out the cupcakes. There wasn't time to start again. Of course, no one knew how this was going to affect the contest round overall. Maybe the judges would give them a few extra minutes at the end? Maybe this round would be canceled? The teams were confused. Everything was chaos.

Leslie announced that the competition was on hold. "All bakers must stay by their kitchens." She then dashed out of the tent.

Henry and Violet found the breaker box. But they weren't the first ones there.

"What's Mr. Lin doing?" Violet asked Henry. The rival bakery owner was closing the box. He stepped back away when, from the other side of the kitchen, Leslie came running up.

Violet and Henry didn't mean to eavesdrop, but Leslie was talking very loudly.

"Is this what you wanted?" Leslie asked Mr. Lin.

"What do you mean?" he asked her. The way he spoke made it sound as if they knew each other well.

"Bad press. So many issues." She rattled off a list of the things that were happening. "Ingredients being switched. Electricity going off. What's going to happen in round three?" she asked.

Mr. Lin shook his head hard. "We need to stop this once and for all."

The Great Greenfield Bake-Off

The two of them hurried away together.

Violet and Henry stepped out of the shadows.

"What was that all about?" Henry asked his sister.

"Sounds like Mr. Lin is involved in the contest problems." She added, "Leslie too."

"I don't want to blame them if it's not their fault," Henry said. "Let's think about all this carefully."

He led her over to the breaker box. Henry knew a lot about electronics. He studied the switches and then said, "There's nothing unusual here."

Trouble in the Tent

"Power's still out," Violet reported. "I wonder what's causing it?"

They found Mrs. Catalan walking around the kitchen platform. She was muttering, "The worst day ever...a disaster...how did this happen?"

"Mrs. Catalan?" Henry said. She looked at him with a frazzled expression. "Can we help?"

"Henry. Violet," she said, sadly. "If the power doesn't come back soon, everyone's desserts will be no good. The day will be ruined." Mrs. Catalan let out a long, ragged breath. "I don't know what to do. I've invested so much money into this event. I thought it was a great idea and would bring new customers to the bakery." She glanced over Henry's shoulder. "Did you see that people are leaving?"

Violet said, "It's just that so many things are going wrong. Some people probably think the contest will be canceled."

"Should I cancel it?" Mrs. Catalan wondered. She wasn't really asking them, just thinking aloud. Then, she shook her head. "Oh, how the bakery would suffer. I might have to close altogether!" She let out a heavy sigh. "This contest was a terrible ide—"

"Wait!" said Henry. He was looking down at the ground. "No need to cancel." Partially buried in the dirt was the end of an extension cord. "Somehow the power to the kitchen got unplugged!"

"Do you think it was on purpose?" Violet asked Mrs. Catalan.

Mrs. Catalan was shocked at what Henry had discovered. "I just don't know what to think anymore." Mrs. Catalan inserted the end of the extension cord into the nearest outlet. The entire contest kitchen whirred as appliances, stove tops, and the ovens came back to life.

Two girls in the back started screaming. Their electric mixer had turned on, and batter was flying everywhere.

"A delicious mess," said Benny. He offered to help.

"The competition is officially back on," Leslie announced. She told the girls that the rules said they had to clean their own messes even if it took extra time and wasn't really their fault.

"That's a bummer rule," Benny said with a sigh. He told Jessie, "Just make a two-people-baking mess, okay? We can't get any helpers."

Jessie agreed that she'd do her best, but just like the electricity going out, there wasn't a lot she could do if things went mysteriously wrong. They didn't have time to talk to Henry and Violet and find out the details. They couldn't leave the baking area. And now they had to get busy baking again.

"I hope nothing else bad happens," Benny said. He peered into the oven. "They still look good! Maybe not quite as extra beautiful. But good!"

"Whew!" Jessie decided to let them bake another minute before calling Leslie over to remove the tin from the oven. "Can you tell us what happened?" Jessie asked while Leslie removed their cupcakes from the oven. No one had explained. Once the power went back on, the competition was the bakers' main focus.

Leslie told them about the extension cord, then said, "Two teams dropped out. Even with the added time we are giving everyone, they didn't think they'd finish. Another team got disqualified for running their cupcakes home to cook them."

She shook her head. "They live nearby, but still, everyone was told to stay at their stations."

"Seven teams are left." Benny held up seven fingers.

"Only three will go on to the finals tomorrow," Leslie said. She paused to watch Jessie scoop ganache over the warm cupcakes. "You seem to be doing well." Jessie set marshmallows on the very top. "Those are the prettiest cupcakes I've seen so far."

"I complimented them," Benny explained. "You have to tell them they're adorable if you want them to be." He whispered so the cupcakes couldn't hear, "It's good for cupcake-confidence."

"Really?" Leslie laughed, maybe for the first time all day.

"It works." Benny nodded.

"We want to make sure they're adorable, plus baked all the way," Jessie said. She asked Leslie to set the cupcakes back in the oven. "Even with the extra time, we need to hurry."

Leslie put the cupcakes in to bake, and Jessie started a timer for five minutes.

Trouble in the Tent

Before she left, Benny told Leslie, "I don't have to tell the cupcakes to be yummy because my tummy tells me that they already are."

"Well, best of luck to you," Leslie said. She started off to help another team with their oven. "I'll be back in a few minutes to take these out for you."

"Four minutes, eight seconds, please," Benny replied after checking the timer.

Connor and Emma had their cupcakes at the end of their workstation, ready to be taken to the judging table before anyone else's. Jessie could hear Connor complaining to the TV crew about the oven problem as she placed her team's finished s'mores cupcakes on a serving platter.

"Power!" he said loudly. "This ragtag contest lost power. Have you ever heard of a competition being run this poorly?"

Even with the issues, Connor had managed to get his cupcakes finished. He went on and on about the electricity for so long that he was still complaining when Leslie announced the judging was about to begin.

The TV crew thanked Connor for the interview

and moved to the judges' table.

"We are here, anxiously awaiting the results of today's second round," the reporter, a tall dark-haired man, said into the camera. The camerawoman told him to move aside so she could get a good view of the judges' faces as they bit into the cupcakes.

The judges carefully examined their cupcakes before they took bites.

Once the judges had tasted each teams' cupcakes, Leslie leaned in to hear Mrs. Catalan whisper in her ear. Daniel Prince was leaning back in his chair and smiling. Merry Holiday had a stern poker face. It was impossible to guess what she was thinking.

"We are not ranking the cupcakes," Leslie said. "The teams that are moving on are all equal from here on." She checked her clipboard.

"Connor and Emma Green. Duke and Daniel Duncan." Those were the twin brothers that Violet knew from art class. "And Jessie and Benny Alden."

"Hurrah!" Henry and Violet were both shouting and cheering from the audience.

Trouble in the Tent

The three teams were invited to the judges' table while the others returned to their stations to pack up their things.

"Your cupcakes were delicious," Daniel Prince told Jessie and Benny.

"But were they adorable?" Benny asked.

"I probably shouldn't tell you this, but they were the most adorable," Mr. Prince whispered.

"They had cupcake-confidence," Benny told Mr. Prince, who didn't really understand what Benny meant.

"He gave a pep talk to the cupcakes," Jessie explained.

Mr. Prince winked. "Ah yes. I do that when I'm baking too."

Benny smiled wide. He started thinking about what he'd like to tell the pie they were making the next day. It had to be beautiful, delicious, creative...oh, there was so much! "I'm going to write a wonderful pie speech," he told Jessie while they walked to where the finalists were going to be photographed for the newspaper.

Connor put himself in the middle of the photo,

not noticing that Emma was stuck behind him. The photographer made him move aside to let her in. He straightened his hat and smiled.

Benny squeezed Jessie's hand.

"What?" She knew it was a sign he had something to tell her.

All he said was, "Leslie."

Jessie saw what he meant. Leslie wasn't waiting for the teams to go home. She wasn't sticking around for cleanup either. The contest assistant was leaving. That wasn't so surprising, but she wasn't walking home. Jessie and Benny could see her running away from the tent and the competition.

"I wonder what the hurry is?" Benny asked.

Jessie didn't have time to answer.

"Say pie!" the photographer called out.

"PIE!"

Who's to Blame?

"So then the power went out." Benny wiped his face with a napkin. "And that's the end of the story from inside the tent."

"There must be more that happened after that," Mrs. McGregor said. The family was at dinner. Grandfather was in his seat at the head of the table. Mrs. McGregor was pouring drinks.

"There's more," Henry said, looking sideways at Benny. He filled everyone in on the breakers, the unplugged extension cord, and the conversation he and Violet had heard between Mr. Lin and Leslie.

"And then we got picked for the next round," Benny said proudly.

"Sounds like an exciting day," Grandfather put in.

"It was fantastic!" Benny looked under the table at Watch. "Sorry you weren't there; you'd have loved it!"

Henry scooped some potatoes onto Benny's plate, then took some for himself. "We're so proud that Jessie and Benny made it to the final. But we should try to figure out who's sabotaging the contest. Mrs. Catalan says that if more things go wrong and the event isn't successful, she might have to close the bakery."

"She put a lot of time and money into the event," Grandfather said. "It's nice of you all to want to help her."

After dinner Jessie, Benny, Violet, and Henry went to the boxcar to discuss the mystery. Watch came along too.

"Well, I already know who is sabotaging the bake-off," Benny said, flopping onto the beanbag chair. "It's that bossy Connor. He's mean to Emma. That makes him our number one suspect."

"Just because he's bossy doesn't mean he's trying to ruin the contest," Jessie said. She sat at her desk and spun her chair around to face Benny.

"Okay, how about this," Benny said. "Connor

was the only one with the right ingredients in round one. Emma went to the bathroom right before the power went off. *And* he's mean." Benny seemed satisfied with his clues. "I think Connor's the one ruining everything."

Violet asked Jessie, "Do you think Connor sabotaged those other teams?" She turned to the others. "Could he have switched the ingredients at every worktable?"

"I don't know," Jessie said. "I don't want to blame Connor without proof." She thought for a moment then said, "Remember that Benny saw Emma with a strange baggie."

"You thought maybe they were bringing their own outside ingredients, but could it have actually been filled with salt?" Henry asked.

"It was a little baggie," Benny admitted. "Not enough to put salt in all the recipes. But that doesn't mean he isn't the bad guy!"

"I suppose he could have made Emma unplug the power," Violet said thoughtfully. She and Henry were on the small couch. "She was missing from the tent when the power went out. And Emma does seem to do anything Connor demands."

"I wonder why," Benny said. "If he were my brother, I'd never do everything he asked."

"Good thing you have a nice brother," Jessie said with a chuckle.

"I feel bad for Emma," Henry remarked. "I hope she figures out how to stand up for herself."

"He wants to win so much that he might cheat," Jessie said. "Then again, he seemed really mad about the tent losing power. Did you hear him complaining to the TV crew?"

"That's true," Henry said. "He was upset. Connor probably wouldn't turn off the power to his own station on purpose."

"But his cupcakes still cooked nicely because they were in the oven and almost done when it happened," Benny reminded them all.

"Are there other suspects?" Jessie asked.

"Nope," Benny said. "Connor did it."

"Really?" Violet asked him. "We can't have a mystery with just one suspect." She pushed Benny to think harder. "Who else might be behind the problems?"

"Mr. Lin," Jessie said.

"He has his own bakery in town, so I don't understand why he's hanging around the bakery competition," said Henry. He repeated the strange conversation Mr. Lin had with Leslie Smallwater. "Leslie asked if this was what he wanted."

"That does seem strange." Jessie began writing notes in her notebook. "Tell me again, Henry, what did Mr. Lin reply?"

"That he'd end it once and for all," Henry said with a shrug. "I don't know what that means."

"That leads us to Leslie Smallwater," Violet said. "She's the third suspect."

"Leslie handles the ingredients," Jessie said. "She even had something on her shirt around the time we discovered the salt and sugar had been swapped."

"She ran away after the competition," Violet put in.

"Leslie knows Mr. Lin," Henry added. "I mean, we all have eaten at his bakery, but she's the one that was talking to him about the contest problems."

"And we know she wanted to be in the contest instead of organizing it," Violet added.

Who's to Blame?

"It does seem like she's hiding something," Jessie agreed. "When she couldn't bake, she offered to organize the contest, but she never acts like she wants to be there. She's always tired and a little grumpy."

"I'm sticking with Connor as suspect number one," Benny said. "He's the bad guy. I know it."

They talked for a few more minutes about suspects and clues, then went back to the kitchen for dessert with Grandfather and Mrs. McGregor.

Tonight's dessert was the practice pie Jessie and Benny had baked. It was blueberry and lemon custard. Jessie had found the recipe in a cookbook high up on Grandfather's shelf. He'd explained that when he was a young boy, he'd loved to bake. His mother had bought him the cookbook. This was one of his favorite pies. Jessie had made some small changes to the recipe, and she and Benny had put delicate almond-paste flowers on top that Violet had taught them to make.

Everyone dove into their pieces of pie. The room became silent.

"You're going to win for certain," Mrs. McGregor

said at last. "This is the best pie I have ever tasted."

"Mmmmm," was all Benny said.

"I'm happy to report that I agree with Mrs. McGregor," Grandfather said. "This pie is incredible!" He laughed. "Better than I ever made it, myself."

"The flowers look great!" Violet said.

Jessie smiled. "Wow. I think we have a chance."

"As long as no one tries to ruin the day," Henry said, "you'll win for sure."

Jessie sighed. "We better figure out this mystery soon."

Benny took her hand as they went to watch the news about the competition. "Don't worry, Jessie. We'll solve it," he whispered. "I'm watching Connor like a hawk!" He pointed at the screen, where Connor was being interviewed by the TV reporter.

This was the recorded interview they'd seen happen live in the baking tent.

Connor was complaining about the power problems and how disorganized the contest seemed. His tall hat filled the TV screen. Emma was in the corner, blocked by her brother.

Who's to Blame?

"I don't like him at all," Benny said.

"That doesn't mean he's sabotaging the contest," Henry reminded Benny. "You don't have to like everyone."

"But I usually do!" Benny said. "I usually like everyone!"

That was true.

"Wait!" Jessie ran over to the TV. They were now showing footage of the bakers at work before the power outage. "Look, Benny, there you are!" The camera showed a close-up of him on the floor telling the cupcakes how adorable they were.

"It worked," Benny bragged. "They were the prettiest. Even Mr. Prince said so." He pointed back to the screen. "There's Jessie mixing."

"Hang on!" Jessie said, moving closer to the TV.

"What is it?" Violet asked.

"It's Leslie," Jessie said. She moved aside so everyone could see. "She's leaving the tent."

"Impossible," Benny said. "She had to put everyone's cupcakes in the oven. She didn't have time to go anywhere."

"Still, she left," Violet said. Then, there on the

news, the camera had caught the lights going out. "I wonder if Leslie forgot something and went to check it out. Or there was something she needed outside the tent." Violet thought of reasons Leslie might leave for a moment.

"Or maybe," Jessie said, "she was the one who turned off the power."

The final image of the story was the photo of the contestants who made it through to the final round. The reporter said, "Good luck to all of our bakers!" Then, the weather report was next.

"There's a lot more we need to find out before we solve this mystery." Henry turned off the TV.

It was time for bed. Tomorrow was going to be a big day!

Pie Problems

"It's the Great Greenfield Bake-Off finale!" Mrs. Catalan announced. The crowd in the stands was much bigger than the day before. Seeing all those people made Jessie nervous. At the same time, she was really happy so many people were there to support Mrs. Catalan.

Benny saw that she was shaking a little. "Bake it with a grin. That's how the Aldens win!"

She nodded and told herself to stay focused on the pie. If she made it just like the practice pie they ate the night before, they'd have a very good chance of winning.

Connor and Emma were making a chocolate pie with fudge ripples.

The Great Greenfield Bake-Off

Duke and Daniel were making a traditional holiday pecan pie with caramel topping.

"The best part of today is that we get to taste everything at the end!" Benny gushed. "I can't wait."

"Let's hope nothing goes wrong," Jessie said.

"Ditto," Benny said, meaning he hoped the same thing. He pulled a rabbit's foot and a penny out of his pocket. "I've got luck for us."

"Good thinking," Jessie said with a smile. "We could use the help!"

"We don't need luck," Connor said. His station was close enough so they could hear each other now. With only three teams in the tent, they'd been moved together for the cameras. He adjusted his hat.

"Is that hat taller than it was yesterday?" Benny asked Connor.

"It just looks taller because his ego is so huge," Emma whispered to Benny.

Connor didn't hear her. Emma shuffled to her place by the mixing bowl.

"Leslie?" Duke called from his station. "It doesn't look like all our ingredients are here."

Pie Problems

"We are missing pecans, which is the most important thing in our pecan pie recipe," Daniel said.

Jessie looked over her own ingredients, which were displayed on the station. "We don't have blueberries," she reported. "The pie needs those."

"We're good," Connor announced. "Nothing is missing. We're ready to begin."

Benny gave Jessie a questioning look. "How come he's got everything?"

Jessie shrugged, reviewing the recipe to see what else might be missing.

Mrs. Catalan hurried over to the tables. She called Leslie over. "Getting the ingredients was your job. Where are the missing things?"

"Probably still in the shopping bags." Leslie pointed to several tote bags in the corner. "I'm still working on it." She yawned. "I never said the contest was ready to go." She yawned again.

"The audience is here. The news crews." Mrs. Catalan was frustrated. "You came to my shop and asked me if you could be the contest assistant. I agreed. I don't understand. Why are you running behind? And why are you so tired?"

The Great Greenfield Bake-Off

"Just give me a few minutes," Leslie said. She brought the blueberries to Jessie and delivered the pecans to the twins. "I think that's everything," Leslie said, pointing at the containers on the stations.

Jessie checked. "Flour, butter, sugar..." There was a brand-new bag of sugar, straight from the store to ensure there were no swaps this time. "Salt, lemons, eggs, and milk." The flower decorations were more difficult. "The marzipan that we will cut into flowers is made of almond paste, powdered sugar, and corn syrup." Jessie turned to Benny. "It's all here. Even the food coloring we requested."

"I'll taste as we go along," Benny said. "Up until you add the eggs. No raw eggs for Benny's belly."

The twins seemed satisfied as well.

With one last big yawn, Leslie asked them, "Are you ready now?"

Each team got a moment to agree. Connor shouted, "I was born for this!" which was his way of saying he was ready. Benny said, "Yes." So did the twins.

"Well then," Leslie said, turning to the contestants. "Bakers, bake!"

Pie Problems

Jessie found the pie tin and began to make the crust. Benny began to squeeze the lemons to get out their juice.

"You two doing okay?" Leslie came by to check.

"So far," said Jessie. "We'll call you when we are ready to put the pie in the oven."

"Good." She went over to the twins, then on to Connor and Emma.

The room was perfectly quiet as everyone concentrated on their pies, until, suddenly, there was a commotion from Connor and Emma's table.

"Connor Green, are you cheating?" Leslie shouted.

Benny tugged on Jessie's apron. "I knew it!"

"Let's find out what's going on," Jessie said. "No one's guilty yet."

Mrs. Catalan and the other two judges hurried to Connor and Emma's table. There was a lot of loud talking.

"I found this baggie on the floor," Leslie told Mrs. Catalan.

"That looks like what I saw yesterday," Benny told Jessie. "What is going on?"

"I'm not cheating," Connor insisted. "I'm improving! These are old family recipes. They need secret ingredients." He looked for the TV camera. "Can you blame me for not wanting to tell everyone my family's secrets?"

"The rules say you can't bring in ingredients on your own," Mrs. Catalan said. "You knew the rules when you signed up."

"You use terrible ingredients!" said Connor. "I can't possibly win without my own spices...I'm going to be a world-famous chef."

"That might be true someday," Mrs. Catalan said. "But right now, in Greenfield, this team is disqualified." All the judges agreed.

"I don't need your competition to succeed," Connor boasted.

Emma paused for a quiet second, then she went and packed up Connor's station before following him out of the tent.

"Well," Jessie remarked when they were gone, "that was a surprise."

"I think the team that was sabotaging the competition just left," Benny said. He stuffed his

lucky penny and rabbit's foot deep into his pocket. "We don't need luck anymore. This tent is safe from mean, cheating bakers!"

"I hope you're right," Jessie said, watching Connor stomp away with Emma behind him. They returned to their own station. "Now we can make our blueberry lemon custard pie without worrying about someone trying to ruin it. Let's start the filling."

CHAPTER 10

The Winner Is...

"Mr. Lin is here again today," Henry told Violet. They'd found good seats in the audience where they could see Jessie and Benny, plus the area around the tent.

"Maybe we should investigate?" Violet suggested. "He's a suspect, after all."

"Connor and Emma got disqualified, so maybe Benny was right," Henry said. "They could have been causing all the trouble." He didn't seem so sure.

"It's never that easy," Violet said. "Maybe Mr. Lin put them up to it?"

"I guess we have to wait and see what happens," Henry said. "Hopefully the trouble is done now that Connor and Emma have left."

The Great Greenfield Bake-Off

"I think there might still be problems," Violet told her brother. She pointed to where the judges were now all gathered around Duke and Daniel's workstation. Jessie and Benny were with Duke and Daniel. Something was clearly wrong at their station too.

Henry saw Mr. Lin glance over at the commotion and start moving around the tent, out of view.

Violet stood. "We have to follow him."

Henry agreed. They came out of the stands and walked the way they'd seen Mr. Lin go. The back of the tent was completely blocked from the audience's view. There wasn't very much back there except a few supply trucks, Mrs. Catalan's van, and the electrical equipment that kept the appliances running. There was also a water truck for pumping water to the sinks.

Henry and Violet were near the edge of the tent when, suddenly, Violet stopped. "What's this?" She bent low to the ground and stuck her finger in a white, powdery mess. The ants were coming quickly, which made Violet realize, "This is sugar."

Henry noticed there was a trail. They began to follow the sugar and the ants...and Mr. Lin.

They found Mr. Lin behind Mrs. Catalan's bakery van. He and Leslie were arguing over something. It looked like a paper bag. Henry squinted at the label.

"That's sugar," he told Violet. "It explains the trail. The bag must be open."

"I wonder what Leslie is doing out here during the event," said Violet.

Mr. Lin grabbed the sugar bag from Leslie's hands, and the entire thing ripped open. Sugar fell in heaps to the dirt. The ants were very excited. They swarmed the sweet treat.

"Where's our sugar?" Henry and Violet heard someone yell from inside the tent.

"The eggs are gone!" another voice said loudly.

Henry and Violet were about to go in to find Jessie and Benny when Jessie and Benny came out to them. The judges came out too. And the twins. And Mrs. Catalan.

"There are ingredients missing from each workstation. We were going to ask Leslie about them, but we couldn't find her and heard voices out here," said Jessie. "The ingredients were there when we checked at the start, and then they disappeared."

"Sugar?" Henry asked. "Is that what's missing?"

"How did you know?" Benny asked.

"We overheard you," Violet explained. Then she pointed to the ground. "I'm guessing that's your missing ingredient all over the place."

"We can't use that," Benny said, making a gross-out face. "It's a gift to the ants."

"And they say, 'Thank you,'" Violet told her brother. "I'm guessing the missing eggs are around here somewhere too."

"Inside the van," said Leslie, who had stopped arguing with Mr. Lin when the judges had come out of the tent. "Mrs. Catalan left the back door open. You'll find the eggs under the seat."

"How do you know?" Benny asked. But he didn't wait for her to answer. He looked at his brother and sisters, then he realized they'd solved the mystery.

Benny gave the answer to his own question. "Oh,

you put the eggs under the seat all by yourself. You were the one trying to ruin the contest!"

Henry listed all the clues that led to Leslie. "First you switched the salt and sugar. There was salt on the back of your clipboard that got all over your shirt. Next, you left the tent so you could turn off the power—we saw that on the news. And now you took ingredients away while everyone was distracted by Connor and Emma's problem."

Leslie nodded. "The distraction was useful to me. I had a plan to sneak the ingredients from each team while I visited the stations to see how things were going," she said. "Connor and Emma made it easier for me." She looked at Mr. Lin. "I was only trying to help you."

Mr. Lin looked confused. "I don't understand how wrecking the contest helps me." He waved his hand over the sugar and pointed to where the eggs were in the van.

"Your bakery is losing customers because of this contest!" she said. "I know because during my evening shifts there have been a lot fewer people coming in. Everyone around town is talking about the new menu item Greenfield Bakery will have after the competition ends." Leslie yawned. "I'm so tired from working here all day and at your bakery at night."

Mr. Lin sighed. "My bakery is struggling." He turned to Mrs. Catalan. "That is why I wanted this to be a joint competition, sponsored by both my bakery and yours. But you said no."

"Did you know Leslie was trying to sabotage the competition?" Henry asked Mr. Lin.

"Absolutely not," Mr. Lin said, shaking his head strongly. He realized what had happened. "But I was complaining about the competition to my wife. I told her, over the phone from my office, that I was worried we'd have to close our bakery if Mrs. Catalan's became more popular."

"I heard that phone call," Leslie said. "I need my job if I want to go to college. I'm saving every penny I make. I work so much, and with homework and school applications, I barely ever sleep anymore. I even have to run from the contest to the bakery." She pointed down at her tennis shoes.

"Running explains why Leslie's so tired all the

time," Benny said. "Running makes me tired too."

Leslie sighed. "So I thought if there was no contest, or a really bad contest, Mrs. Catalan wouldn't get new customers, and Mr. Lin's bakery would survive. At first I wanted to join the bake-off. My idea was that if I won, I could tell everyone where I worked, and then Mr. Lin would get new customers."

"But you were too late to sign up," Violet said, remembering when Leslie came into the bakery to enter the competition.

"Work was busy," said Leslie. "I couldn't get away in time."

"So you asked to be the assistant," Jessie said. "And made a new plan."

Leslie nodded. "I'm really sorry. I was just so worried."

"I am sorry too." Mr. Lin put his hand on her shoulder. "I let you think you needed to do something drastic to help me."

The mystery was all coming together. But Henry still had one question. He explained that he and Violet had heard Mr. Lin and Leslie arguing outside the tent. "When you said, 'We need to stop this,' what did that mean?"

"I meant stop the things from going wrong," Mr. Lin said. "That's why I came back today. I was going to try to solve the mystery."

"You should leave mysteries to us," Benny said. "It's our specialty."

"I'll remember that next time," Mr. Lin said with a laugh.

"I'm sorry too," Mrs. Catalan put in. "Next year we should host the Great Greenfield Bake-Off together. I was being selfish. I don't want your bakery to go out of business." She smiled. "Competition is good. It makes us all work a little harder."

Mr. Lin and Mrs. Catalan shook hands. Everyone returned to the bake-off tent, where they were greeted with one more surprise.

Connor came running into the tent with Emma by his side. "Can I be sorry too?" he asked.

"I'm also sorry to Conner and all the contestants," Emma said. "I was so mad at my brother for signing me up with him. I didn't want to help at all."

The Great Greenfield Bake-Off

"Then why did you?" Violet asked.

"Our mom is a pastry chef, and he wanted to show off to her what he knew." She frowned. "No matter what he did, Mom was still too busy to notice. We decided together that we had to win to get her attention, so we did a very bad thing."

"That's why you added your own ingredients?" Jessie asked.

"Yes," Connor said. "I thought if I won, Mom would be extra proud." He looked to the audience where a woman stood, waving. "Turns out she was already proud. She was just so busy with work that she didn't realize what was going on. She's going to spend more time with me and Emma now."

"I'm sorry I was mean," Connor told Emma.

"And I'm sorry we cheated," he said to everyone.

Jessie thought about all that happened during the competition. Now she knew that Connor and Emma had brought in special ingredients. But something still didn't add up. It hadn't been sugar that Benny had seen in a baggie during the first round. "How did your cheesecake turn out so well?" Jessie asked.

The Winner Is...

"At the beginning, I was mad at the way my brother was treating me, so I didn't put any sugar in our pumpkin cheesecake," Emma confessed. "Our sugar had been switched by Leslie too, only we didn't use it, so we didn't know! We won by accident because it wasn't too salty."

"I thought she ruined the dessert, but she saved it," Connor said, pulling his sister in for a hug.

"Can we finish the competition?" Leslie asked Mrs. Catalan. "This time I'll get all the pie ingredients and be ready on time."

"Next time you have a problem, you come talk to me, okay?" Mr. Lin told Leslie.

"Yes," Leslie said. "I will."

Mrs. Catalan stood quietly. She looked around at everyone while trying to decide what they should do. Finally, she said, "The final bake-off is between Duke and Daniel and Jessie and Benny. The best pie will win the day." No one moved. "Go!" she said, pointing at the kitchen stations. "Leslie, get the ingredients they need. We'll start in ten minutes."

The audience cheered.

Henry and Violet returned to the audience.

The Great Greenfield Bake-Off

Grandfather and Watch and Mrs. McGregor had come to see the end of the competition. Mr. Lin sat with Connor and Emma and their mom. The mystery had been solved, and now it was time to see which team would win.

***

Duke and Daniel Duncan won the day. Their pecan pie was thick and had just the right amount of pecans. The judges loved Jessie and Benny's blueberry lemon custard pie, but they chose the Duncan twins' pie to be the grand winner.

After announcing that the Duncan Pie would be the new menu item at Greenfield Bakery, Mrs. Catalan had something else to say. "Even though Team Alden didn't win the competition, they helped *save* the competition. Mr. Lin and I want to say a special thank you to Jessie, Benny, Henry, and Violet."

"I think we got the best award," Benny said happily.

While the twins got their picture taken for the newspaper, Benny finally got to taste something from the competition. He was holding the pecan pie in one hand. There was caramel topping on his chin.

"This is a really great pie," Benny told Jessie, Henry, and Violet. "Ours was good too, but this is really amazing!" He thought about pies. "Can we do the contest again next year? I think we should make a strawberry, chocolate, coconut, pineapple, and marshmallow pie."

"With nuts or no nuts?" Violet asked seriously.

Jessie got a pen and paper to write down the recipe.

"Yes, nuts for sure," Benny said. He thought some more. "And whipped cream, and caramel, and apples, and peaches, and ice cream and sprinkles..." Benny kept adding ingredients for his pie, on and on, until he finally said, "With a cherry on top."

Turn the page to read a
sneak preview of

THE BEEKEEPER MYSTERY

the new
Boxcar Children mystery!

Benny Alden lay on his back, staring at the living room ceiling. Watch, the family's wirehaired terrier, was curled next to him. It was the last week of summer vacation. Benny was wondering what he and his siblings would do this week when the phone rang.

"Can somebody please get that?" called Grandfather.

Benny scrambled up and answered the phone. "Hello?" he said.

"Benny?" asked a woman. Benny thought the voice sounded familiar. "It's Laura," she said. "Laura Shea. I know we've talked about a visit to the farm, and I wondered if you and your siblings could come this week. Are you busy?"

"No," said Benny. "We're just waiting for school to start."

"Perfect," said Laura. "I could really use your

help with an emergency. A honeybee emergency!"

***

"I've never heard of a honeybee emergency," said Jessie Alden. The twelve-year-old girl rode in the back seat of the car with her six-year-old brother, Benny, and ten-year-old sister, Violet. They were on their way to Laura's farm. Her big brother, Henry, sat up front with Grandfather. "What exactly *is* a honeybee emergency?" Jessie asked.

"I don't know," said Benny. "But Laura needs our help."

"Well," said Violet, "it sounds really important."

Up front, Henry looked at the road map. The fourteen-year-old was telling Grandfather which roads to take to the farm.

The children liked taking road trips to new places. Laura and David Shea used to live near the Aldens in Greenfield. They owned the children's favorite restaurant, Applewood Café. Laura let the children help care for the restaurant's vegetable garden. Then the Sheas bought a farm and moved from Connecticut to New York.

"I miss Applewood's hamburgers with honey-barbeque sauce," said Henry.

Violet retied the purple bow on one of her ponytails. "I miss their pancakes with honey and powdered sugar," she said.

"I miss everything," said Benny.

"Look," said Grandfather. A big highway sign ahead said: Welcome to New York—The Empire State.

Soon they were passing open country fields. "I wish Watch could've come," said Benny. "He could run around without a leash."

"That," said Jessie, "is *exactly* why Laura asked us to leave Watch at home with Mrs. McGregor." Mrs. McGregor was their housekeeper. She took care of Watch when the family was away. "Bees and dogs just don't mix," Jessie said. "Watch would get into all sorts of trouble. Remember the time he chased that skunk?"

"P U!" said Benny, holding his nose.

"Take the next exit," Henry told Grandfather. "Then turn right."

Grandfather turned off the highway onto a narrow country road. Benny bounced in his seat.

"Are we there, are we there?"

"Almost," said Henry.

The children once lived near a small road like this. After their parents died, they were scared to go live at their grandfather's house. They'd never met him before. What if he was mean? They ran away and hid in the woods. One night they found shelter from a thunderstorm in an old railroad car hidden among the trees. That boxcar became their new home. Then one day their grandfather found them. Grandfather turned out to be a kind, loving man. He asked them to live with him, and they'd lived together happily ever since.

"We're here," said Henry. They drove under a sign that said: Applewood Farm. Grandfather pulled up to an old farmhouse and everyone scrambled out. Henry unloaded their bags from the trunk.

"You can't park there!" A tall gray-haired woman marched toward them. "This is private property. Parking for the store is down the road."

"Oh," said Grandfather. "Laura asked us—"

An old, red truck rumbled up. Benny's eyes grew

wide. The driver was dressed in all white—almost like an astronaut! Their head was even covered by a hat and veil. The person in the white spacesuit climbed out, calling, "Hello! Welcome!" As the hat with the veil came off, long black hair tumbled out.

"Laura!" cried Jessie.

Laura spread her arms wide for a group hug. "I am so happy to see you all," she said.

The gray-haired woman crossed her arms, frowning. "You know these people?" she asked.

"The Aldens are dear friends," said Laura. "They've come to help harvest our honey." She turned to the children, saying, "Everyone, this is my new neighbor, Zelda. She moved here from the city and took my beekeeping class last month. She's volunteered to help with our honey harvest too."

Zelda walked away, muttering, "Beekeeping is much too difficult for children."

Laura grinned at the children. "Oh, how I've missed you."

"You told Benny you have an emergency," said Henry. "How can we help?"

"Actually," said Laura, "I have two emergencies."

She pulled off her gloves. "First, I'm starting a beekeeping class in two weeks for local children. But I've never taught children before. I thought since I know you all so well, I could practice my teaching on you. My second emergency is that David was called away on business. He'll be gone all week. I really, *really* need your helping hands to harvest our honey."

Jessie twirled a lock of her straight brown hair around and around her finger. "Will we work with real, live honeybees?" she asked.

"Of course," said Laura.

"Will we wear spacesuits like yours?" asked Benny.

Laura ruffled Benny's hair. "Absolutely!" she said. "Except these are beekeeping suits."

"Count us in!" said Henry.

Laura gave them high-fives. "Thank you, thank you, thank you," she said. "You'll start after lunch. Right now, I have to check a few things in the pasture. You can go inside and unpack. There's a room at the top of the stairs with bunk beds that I fixed up for you. I'll send Walt over to give you a tour. He knows this farm better than anyone. We'll meet back here for lunch."

Grandfather smiled. "I can see you don't need me. Laura, it's wonderful to see you again. I know the children are in good hands." He hugged his grandchildren good-bye. "I have work to do back home," he said. "I'll see you all at the end of the week."

After Grandfather left, the children quickly unpacked. Then they went back outside. They were eager to see more of the farm. A man wearing faded-blue overalls and scuffed work boots stood waiting for them. His bushy, white eyebrows and wavy white hair reminded Benny of Santa Clause. "I'm Walt," he said in a booming voice. "Laura asked me to show you around. Let's go."

Walt took long strides. They hurried to catch up. "Do you work here?" asked Henry.

Walt grunted. "This was *my* farm for fifty years," he said. "'Til I got too old. Laura and David came along and bought the place. I tried sittin' around my house all day doin' a whole lot of nothin'. But I got bored."

"I hate being bored," said Benny.

Walt looked at the little boy with the brown hair as if noticing him for the first time. Walt grunted, then said, "I asked the Sheas if they needed help. And here I am."

Walt showed them Applewood's vegetable garden, tall rows of corn, pumpkin patch, and fields of wildflowers. In the distance, stands of colored boxes stood along a fence. "Those are some of our beehives," said Walt. "There's more in the next pasture." He looked at the children. "Can't say I approve of putting kids and bees together."

"Didn't your children help with *your* bees?" Henry asked.

"Never did have kids," said Walt. "Don't know much about 'em."

"Oh!" Violet clasped her hands. "What's that?" A little, white building with purple trim and a purple door stood near the road. Purple flowers grew all around. Purple was Violet's favorite color in the whole world.

"Gift shop," said Walt.

"It's so pretty," said Violet. "Can we see inside? Please?"

A bell tinkled as they entered. The children walked slowly around the small shop. There were jars of honey, baskets with honey-made soaps, honey body creams and lip balms, and boxes of honey granola, trail mix, and cereal bars.

A heavyset teenage boy was stacking cookbooks on a shelf. His bee-shaped name tag said: NOAH. "Can I help you?" he asked.

"Is everything here made with honey?" asked Benny.

Noah looked around. "Not the cookbooks," he said. "Or the tee shirts. Are you taking Walt's farm tour?"

"We are," said Violet. "This shop is my favorite so far."

"Have..." Noah's voice grew shaky, "have you seen the bees?"

"We're seeing them after lunch," said Henry.

Benny grinned. "We get to wear spacesuits! Um, *bee* suits."

Noah gulped. "Be careful...you don't want to get stung."

"We'll be careful," Jessie said. She wondered

why Noah worked so close to bees when he was obviously afraid of them.

Walt lifted a bushy, white eyebrow. "Good grief, Noah," he said. "Don't go making people afraid of bees. Honeybees are just about the most amazing insects on the whole planet. You've never even *visited* our hives." Walt turned to the Aldens. "Let's go," he said, "time for lunch."

They reached the farmhouse just as Laura drove in from the field. Her face looked tight with worry. "There's a tear in the fence near the hives," she said, climbing out of the truck.

"Are the hives okay?" asked Walt.

Laura nodded. "They look okay."

The old farmer scratched his chin. "Could be a branch fell on the fence during that storm last night." He climbed into the red truck. "I'll go mend it."

Laura turned to the children. Her troubled face eased into a smile. "Anyone hungry?" she asked.

"Me!" said Benny.

"I thought so." She laughed.

GERTRUDE CHANDLER WARNER discovered when she was teaching that many readers who like an exciting story could find no books that were both easy and fun to read. She decided to try to meet this need, and her first book, *The Boxcar Children*, quickly proved she had succeeded.

Miss Warner drew on her own experiences to write the mystery. As a child she spent hours watching trains go by on the tracks opposite her family home. She often dreamed about what it would be like to set up housekeeping in a caboose or freight car—the situation the Alden children find themselves in.

While the mystery element is central to each of Miss Warner's books, she never thought of them as strictly juvenile mysteries. She liked to stress the Aldens' independence and resourcefulness and their solid New England devotion to using up and making do. The Aldens go about most of their adventures with as little adult supervision as possible—something else that delights young readers.

Miss Warner lived in Putnam, Connecticut, until her death in 1979. During her lifetime, she received hundreds of letters from girls and boys telling her how much they liked her books.